Gemini had a secret.

Gemini had found a little fluffy monster.

The monster was called Whisper.

Gemini saw Whisper in the neighbour's garden on the way home from school.

Whisper followed Gemini home.

"How was school today,
Gemini? Is that something under your
coat?" called Mum from the kitchen.

"Fine thanks! No Mum!" shouted Gemini,
rushing upstairs to hide Whisper.

Gemini felt that Whisper had to be hidden, or people might be angry. Gemini made the decision not to tell ANYONE.

"Let's make you a bed in this shoebox, Whisper. It will be really cosy and if I hide it under my bed no one will EVER find you!"

Gemini liked having a secret. A secret from parents, a secret from brothers and a secret from baby sisters.

This made Gemini feel special.

Mum shouted up the stairs:
"Your dinner's ready Gemini!"

It made Gemini jump! Gemini quickly
hid Whisper away under the bed and
ran downstairs.

"So... how was your day today Gemini? You haven't spoken to anyone since you got home!" asked Mum.

"It was fine, nothing happened..." replied Gemini.

Gemini felt strange. Gemini had NEVER kept a secret from everyone before.

"Can I go out and play now?" asked Gemini, jumping up to leave.

"Yes, but go and put a coat on!" shouted Mum as Gemini ran off.

Gemini rushed to check on Whisper and get a coat.

Something very strange had happened. Whisper no longer fitted in the shoebox. Whisper had grown!

Gemini ignored it, thinking it was impossible, and went to play outside to meet Jack.

Jack was Gemini's best friend.

"What did you do when you got back from school today?" asked Jack.

"Nothing. Let's go and play in your garden!" said Gemini.

Gemini felt strange... again. Gemini had kept a secret from Jack!

When Gemini got home, Gemini
sneaked upstairs, so no one would ask
any questions.

As soon as Gemini got into the bedroom,
something wasn't right.

Something smelt funny.

Whisper was HUGE.

Whisper didn't even fit under the bed anymore!

And what's more, Gemini started to feel sad and scared.

Gemini had a secret. A secret from parents, a secret from brothers and a secret from baby sisters.

But Gemini didn't feel special any more. Gemini had hidden Whisper from EVERYONE.

And every time Gemini wasn't honest Whisper had got bigger, hairier and smellier.

Gemini was worried. It was time someone was told about this secret.

But who..?

Mum? Dad? A teacher? Jack?

Gemini decided to tell Jack. Jack was a very good friend and would be able to help Gemini tell someone they could trust.

If Jack helped Gemini tell someone they could trust, it wouldn't be so scary!

So Gemini told Jack, who agreed to help.

When Gemini and Jack went to get Whisper, Gemini realised Whisper had already got a bit smaller.

Gemini also noticed it didn't feel as scary anymore now that someone knew about the secret.

Gemini and Jack wheeled Whisper to the living room, where Gemini's Mum sat.

Gemini told Mum EVERYTHING. And as the secret was told, Whisper got smaller and smaller. And less smelly!

Gemini felt so much better after telling Mum the secret. It had been hard to keep the secret from family and friends. Gemini had felt sad, worried and scared.

Plus, Whisper wouldn't have got so big, hairy and smelly!

Mum said: "The longer you keep a secret, the bigger and scarier it gets until you can't hide it anymore. That's why it's better to just tell someone straight away!"